W9-CCH-787

Gift of the Knapp Foundation
2002-2003

Earth's Changing Mountains

by Neil Morris

Raintree

Chicago, Illinois

LIBRARY
FRANKLIN PIERCE COLLEGE
RINDGE NH 03461

© Copyright 2004 Raintree
Published by Raintree, a division of Reed Elsevier, Inc.
Chicago, IL 60602
Customer Service 888-363-4266
Visit our website at www.raintreelibrary.com

All rights reserved. No part of this book may be reproduced or utilized in any form or by any means, electronic or mechanical, including photocopying, recording, or by any information storage and retrieval system, without permission in writing from the Publishers. Inquiries should be addressed to:

For more information address the publisher Raintree, 100 N. LaSalle, Suite 1200, Chicago IL 60602

Printed and bound in China by South China Printing Company
07 06 05 04 03
10 9 8 7 6 5 4 3 2 1

Editorial: Keith Ulrich
Design: Erica Barraca
Picture Services: Michelle Lisseter and Bridge Creative Ltd
Illustrations: Bridge Creative Services Ltd
Production: Sal D'Amico

Cover photograph of mountains in Bern, Switzerland, with permission of Eye Ubiquitous (Jill Swainson).

The publishers would like to thank Margaret Mackintosh for her assistance in the preparation of this book.

Every effort has been made to contact copyright holders of any material reproduced in this book. Any omissions will be rectified in subsequent printings if notice is given to the publishers.

Library of Congress Cataloging-in-Publication Data

Morris, Neil, 1946-
  Earth's changing mountains / Neil Morris.
     p. cm. -- (Landscapes and people)
Summary: Looks at the geography and people that make up mountain regions throughout the world, focusing on the changing characteristics of both. Includes bibliographical references (p.   ) and index.
 ISBN 1-4109-0174-2 (hc), 1-4109-0345-1 (pb)
 1. Mountains--Juvenile literature. 2. Landscape changes--Juvenile literature. 3. Mountain ecology--Juvenile literature. 4. Nature--Effect of human beings on--Juvenile literature. [1. Mountains. 2. Landscape changes. 3. Mountain ecology. 4. Ecology. 5. Nature--Effect of human beings on.] I. Title. II. Series: Morris, Neil, 1946-   Landscapes and people.
GB512.M65 2003
910'.914'3--dc21

                              2003002180

Acknowledgments
The publishers would like to thank the following for permission to reproduce photographs: p. 17 Alamy Images; p. 4, 13 Phil Schermeister/Corbis, p. 15, 24, 27 Sygma/Jacques Langevin/Corbis; p. 21, 23 Stone/Getty Images; p. 9 Richard Revels/Natural Science Photos, p. 12 Pete Oxford/Natural Science Photos, p. 18 Pete Oxford/Natural Science Photos; p. 10 Daryl Balfour/NHPA, p. 16 Nigel J. Dennis/NHPA, p. 26 A.N.T/NHPA; p. 6 Harold E. Wilson/Oxford Scientific Films, p. 20 Colin Monteath/Oxford Scientific Films, p. 25 David Simonson/Oxford Scientific Films, p. 29 Rick Price/SAL/Oxford Scientific Films.

Contents

Any words appearing in the text in bold, **like this,** are explained in the Glossary.

What Are Mountains?

What do you think of when you think of a mountain? Is it steep and rocky, with daring climbers clinging to its sides as they slowly make their way to the top? Or is it full of grassy slopes, where sheep graze and colorful mountain flowers grow? Whichever one you think of, you're right. A mountain can be both of these things, and many others, too.

All mountains are parts of Earth's surface that stand high above their surroundings. Smaller rises are usually called hills. Some mountains are very steep and form high, pointed **peaks.** Others have a more rounded shape, though the top of these mountains may be just as high.

A mountain may be a single peak, but mountains are often joined together in a mountain **range.** Some ranges have hundreds of separate peaks. When ranges are grouped together, they are sometimes called a mountain **chain.**

At 6,290 feet (1,917 meters), Mt. Washington is the highest peak in New Hampshire. This mountain is in the Presidential Range, which forms part of the larger White Mountains chain. They both belong to a mountain system called the Appalachians.

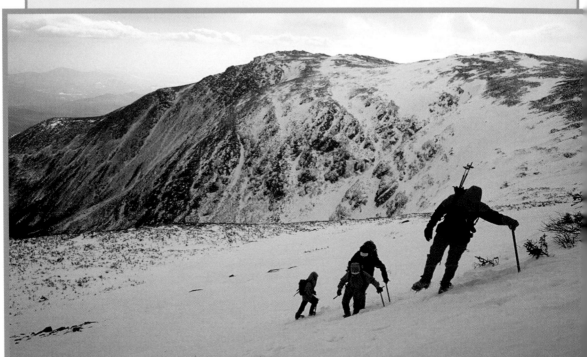

World of mountains

There are mountains all over the world, with major ranges on every **continent.** There is even a high mountain range in Antarctica, the icy continent that lies around the South Pole. It stretches 2,200 miles (3,500 kilometers) across the frozen land.

> *This world map shows the location of the ten longest mountain ranges. The longest of all, the Andes, stretches for 4,470 miles (7,200 kilometers) down the length of South America. Its peaks form parts of seven different countries.*

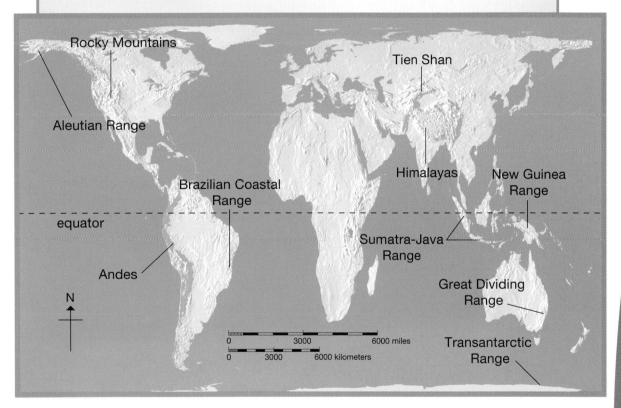

Looking at mountains

In this book we look at the different features of mountains and the way in which they change over time. Mountains are formed in different ways and are shaped by wind and weather. There are many different kinds of mountains, including explosive **volcanoes,** which can cause major changes in the surrounding **landscape.**

People live on, use, and change mountains as well. In recent years **industry** and **tourism** have had a great effect on many of the world's mountain ranges. In some places this has caused problems.

5

How Are Mountains Formed?

Mountains are formed over long periods of time by the movement of rocks beneath the earth's surface. This surface is part of our planet's rocky outer layer, which is called the **crust.** This crust is not one continuous layer, like the shell of an egg, but is broken into several huge pieces. We call these pieces **tectonic plates.**

Jigsaw of plates

Earth's plates fit together like a giant jigsaw, with the sides of each plate close up against other plates. The plates are not still—they are always moving, very slowly, by just a few inches each year. This means that some edges of the plates push against each other, and as they do, they buckle (bend) at the edges. Over many thousands of years, this pressing and bending pushes mountains up from the earth's surface.

Volcanoes

Beneath the earth's crust there is a thick layer called the mantle. The rocks here are so hot that some of them have melted, making them runny like warm taffy. In some places where one plate is forced beneath another, the hot, **molten** rock forces its way through a crack in the earth's crust and forms an erupting **volcano.** Once it is on the surface, the molten rock cools and hardens again. If this goes on happening at the same spot for many thousands of years, the cooled material builds up to form a volcanic cone or a mountain. When a volcano has not erupted for many years, it is said to be dormant, or "sleeping." After thousands of years, it may be called extinct, or "dead"—but the mountains formed by these volcanoes still remain.

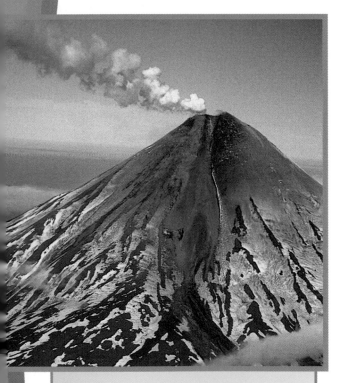

This active, smoking volcano lies on one of the Aleutian islands of Alaska. The islands are part of the Ring of Fire (see page 7).

Shifting ground

There are many volcanoes around the edge of the Pacific Ocean. This circle of tectonic plate boundaries around the Pacific is called the **Ring of Fire** (see the map below). Throughout this whole area, erupting volcanoes often change the **landscape.** In 1980, for example, a volcano in the Cascade Range in Washington State erupted. A huge explosion blew 1,300 feet (400 meters) off the top of Mount St. Helens. The surrounding area was covered in volcanic ash and rock. Before that day, Mount St. Helens had been dormant for 123 years.

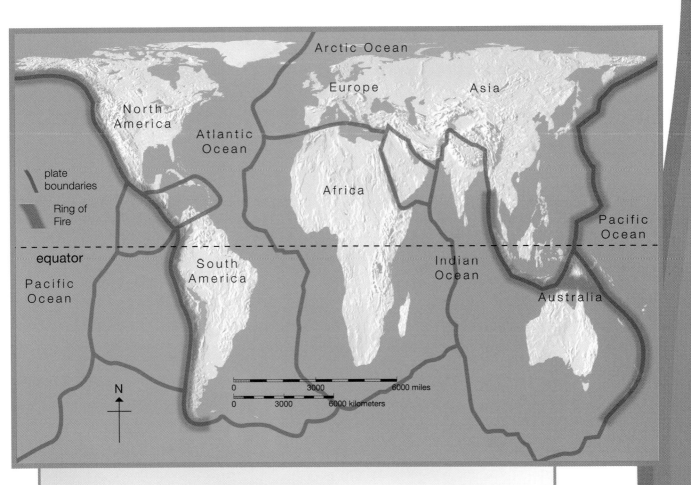

Arctic Ocean

Europe **Asia**

North America

Atlantic Ocean

plate boundaries

Ring of Fire

Africa

Pacific Ocean

equator

Pacific Ocean

South America

Indian Ocean

Australia

N

| 0 | | 3000 | | 6000 miles |
| 0 | 3000 | | 6000 kilometers | |

*This map shows the world's major plates. As the plates move—very, very slowly—they change the shape of **continents** and create mountains. There are mountain ranges on the ocean floor, too. A huge range called the Mid-Atlantic Ridge stretches right down the middle of the Atlantic Ocean. Here the plates are moving apart, allowing molten rock to force its way through and form mountains.*

Folds and faults

Earth's **plates** are made up of layers of rock. As the plates move, the layers of rock are squeezed and crumpled into folds. The world's biggest mountain **ranges** were all made this way over millions of years. Some of them, such as the Himalayas, are still being folded and pushed up. This means they get a tiny bit higher every year.

Sometimes the rock layers are pushed and folded so much that they cannot bend any more. Then they break and form a crack called a **fault.** Different kinds of mountains, including **volcanoes,** form along a fault.

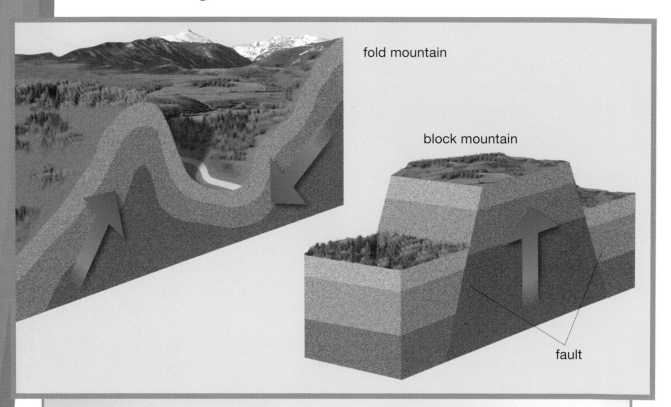

fold mountain

block mountain

fault

As mountains fold up (left), they leave valleys between them. Fold mountains have pointed or rounded peaks. Block mountains appear between faults in the surface of the earth, and usually have a flat top.

Different shapes

Fold mountains are caused by squeezing and crumpling. The top parts of the folds become mountains, and the lower parts between them are **valleys.** The Appalachians in the eastern United States (see page 13), are fold mountains. So are the European Alps, which are much younger. They formed about 50 million years ago.

When a piece of the earth's crust fractures (cracks), layers of rock are sometimes pushed up between two faults. These are called block (or fault-block) mountains. Examples are the Teton Range in Wyoming, which formed about 10 million years ago, and the Harz Mountains in Germany, which are much older.

Dome mountains are formed when the top layers of the earth's crust are pushed up by **molten** rock underneath. This creates a big bulge, or dome, on the surface. The Black Hills in South Dakota, pushed up about 65 million years ago, are dome mountains.

*Layers of rock are called **strata.** It is easy to see here how the strata have been squeezed and folded on the south coast of England. Rocks are very hard materials, so imagine the force that was needed to change these strata.*

Changing Landscapes

Air cools as it rises, so the higher the mountain, the colder the temperature at its **peak.** This is why high mountains are covered in snow, even in the hottest parts of the world. In the East African country of Tanzania, the climate is hot and tropical. Yet the country's highest mountain, Kilimanjaro, is so high (19,300 feet/5,895 meters) that it is cold enough for snow to stay at the top all year round.

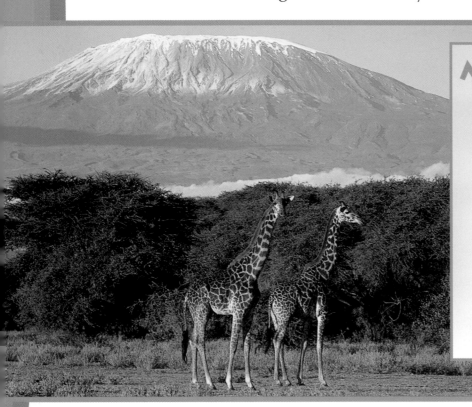

Mount Kilimanjaro, in East Africa, is a dormant volcano. Although it is very cold at the top of the mountain, the lower slopes make good farming land. Kilimanjaro is surrounded by wildlife parks in Tanzania and Kenya.

Rain shadow

High mountain **ranges** affect rainfall in surrounding regions. This is because winds in mountainous regions usually blow from one direction, bringing clouds with them. As the clouds rise to pass over the mountains, they cool and drop rain or snow on the slopes below. This means that the windward side of a mountain—the slope that has the wind blowing toward it—is often wet. When the winds reach the other side, they have lost their moisture and are dry. Because of this, the leeward, or sheltered, side of a mountain where the wind is blowing away receives much less rain. We call this a rain shadow.

moist wind from sea

air cools as it rises

dry wind

rain shadow

desert

equator

PACIFIC OCEAN

Andes Mountains

Patagonian Desert

N

| 0 | 500 | 1000 miles |
| 0 | 500 | 1000 kilometers |

As moist winds from the Pacific Ocean pass over the western side of the Andes Mountains in South America, it often rains. On the eastern side of the mountains, the air no longer holds enough water to rain. In this region of southern Argentina, the rain shadow has helped to create the dry Patagonian Desert.

Mountain winds

As wind flows down mountain slopes, it warms quickly. In the European Alps, a dry wind blows down the northern slopes. As the wind warms, it can cause snow to melt and slide down the mountainside in dangerous **avalanches.** On the eastern side of the Rocky Mountains, similar mountain winds are known as chinooks (and sometimes as snow eaters). A chinook that drops 3,300 feet (1,000 meters) down a mountain may warm up by as much as 50° F (10° C). This makes it easy to understand why areas that have chinook winds are generally warm.

Weathering

Mountains change over long periods of time. Some mountain **ranges** are still being pushed higher by **tectonic plate** movements, while others are very slowly becoming smaller. Their **peaks** are lower than they once were, because the effects of weather have worn them away. Wind, rain, and ice gradually break down rocks in a process called **weathering.** Eventually, small pieces of rock are carried away down the mountain.

Rain and snow

Water causes many changes to mountain **landscapes.** It is cold near the top of a high mountain. This means that there is often a lot of snow rather than rainfall, and any running water quickly freezes. It often freezes in cracks in rocks. Water expands when it freezes and splits the rock, which helps break it into little pieces. Lower down the mountain, where it is usually warmer, water runs in tiny streams, which flow together to make rivers. The force of the moving water washes away pieces of rock, carrying them down the mountain.

This glacier is moving down from high mountain peaks in southwest Argentina.

Rivers of ice

Near the top of some mountains, snow piles up in the cold air and turns to ice. Eventually, the thick layer of ice begins to slide slowly down the side of the mountain. It forms a river of ice, called a **glacier.** Many glaciers travel less than 3 feet (1 meter) a day, but as they move, they drag pieces of rock with them. The rocks, **boulders,** and stones grind against the mountain beneath the glacier. Over thousands of years, the glacier cuts a deeper and deeper U-shaped **valley** in the mountain.

Old mountains

The Appalachian Mountains stretch for about 1,490 miles (2,400 kilometers) down the eastern side of the U.S. They were squeezed up around 300 million years ago and are the oldest mountains in North America. Scientists believe that the Appalachians were formed when plates moved toward each other and caused rock layers to fold up (see page 8). When they first formed, the mountains must have had high, jagged peaks. In the millions of years since then, however, the peaks have been **eroded,** making them more smooth and rounded. The range's highest point is 6,700 feet (2,037 meters) above **sea level** at the top of Mount Mitchell in North Carolina.

Changing Life

Imagine you are a mountaineer, climbing to the highest **peaks** of a mountain. On your way to the top, you would see that growing conditions for plants change. These conditions change with the seasons, too. On mountains, just as lower down, most plant growth takes place in spring and summer. Then the days are long and warm. In winter it is generally too cold for plants to grow, especially on the higher slopes.

The forest zone

The lowest slopes of the mountain (known as the forest zone) may be warm enough for **broad-leaved trees,** such as oak and ash, to grow. These kinds of trees need warm summers and mild winters, so they cannot grow higher up the mountain where the weather is colder. Instead, the upper part of the forest zone is often covered with **conifers,** such as pine and fir. These evergreen trees have strong, needle-shaped leaves, and their roots spread out well in the thin soil. They can survive long winters, when the slopes are frozen hard. Where trees have been cut down, there may be grassy **alpine meadows.** Mountain farmers use these meadows for grazing their animals.

The forest zone is below the tree line. Only small plants grow above the tree line. Bare rock leads up to the snow line. Higher than this, there is always snow.

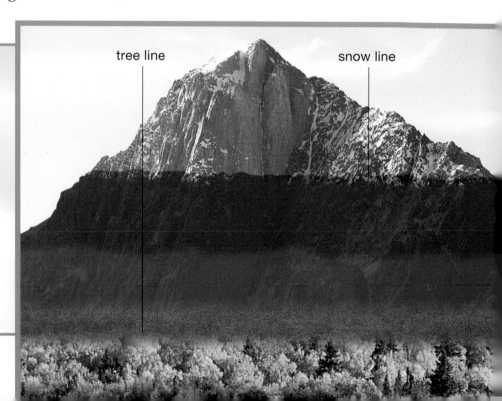

tree line

snow line

Above the tree line

The upper limit of the forest zone is called the **tree line** (or timber line). Above this level it is too cold and windy for trees to live. Most soil here is quickly blown away. Only tough grasses and low, flowering alpine plants grow above the tree line. Higher still you will find only mosses and lichens growing.

Above the snow line

High mountains have snow on their peaks year round. Above a certain level, called the **snow line,** there is always a layer of snow on the slopes. In warm regions of the world, the snow line is very high up. Mount Kilimanjaro in tropical Africa (see page 10) is a good example of this. In colder regions, near the North and South Poles, the snow line is lower down the mountain.

These tough conditions affect animals, trees, and plants because there is very little food for them on mountains. For the same reason, people rarely live above the lower slopes.

These cows are grazing on an alpine meadow in Switzerland. There is snow on the peaks, and the animals move down the mountain in winter (see page 21).

Adapting to the mountains

Some animals have **adapted** to life in the difficult conditions of the mountains. Many, such as mountain goats, have a thick coat to keep them warm during the severe winter. Mountain goats are able to climb along rocky **crags,** but they move down to the lower slopes in winter. Other animals, such as alpine marmots, don't move down the slopes, but dig burrows and sleep through the winter. Mountain hares and some birds have coats or feathers that change color during winter from brown to white so that they are not easily seen by **predators** against the snowy background.

The lammergeier, or bearded vulture, lives in the Pyrenees Mountains of Europe as well as the Himalayas. It is famous for breaking open the bones of dead animals it finds on the slopes. The lammergeier carries a bone up to a great height and drops it onto rocks below, splitting it open to get at the juicy marrow inside.

Mountain cats

Two of the world's big cats have adapted to life in the mountains. Mountain lions (also called pumas or cougars) are found in North and South America, but they have become rare wherever people have taken over the **landscape.** Pumas in the United States live in the western mountains. They are quite happy at high **altitude,** and have been found on mountains 15,000 feet (4,500 meters) high.

The snow leopard lives, as you can guess, in the cold mountains of central Asia. It is at home on rocky slopes, ice, and snow. It has long, thick fur to keep it warm. High up in the cold mountains, the snow leopard hunts wild goats, small musk deer, and a type of wild sheep known as blue sheep. In heavy snow and very cold weather, a snow leopard will move down into the **valleys** to find food.

Ox of Tibet

The yak is a wild ox of Asia. It lives high up in the mountains of Tibet, where winter temperatures drop well below freezing. It is a big animal that measures up to 6 feet (1.8 meters) high at the shoulders, with long horns. It is used to living on the mountains and, despite its size, is light-footed and can slide down icy slopes. Many years ago the farmers of the region (see page 20) realized that the yak could be useful to them in many ways. They use yaks to carry heavy loads, and also keep them for their milk.

Llamas are used to carry loads in the Andes of South America.

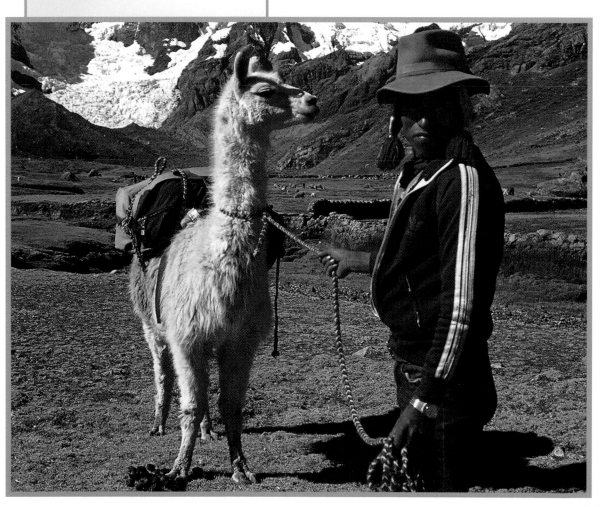

Changing Settlements

You might think that people would not want to live high up in the mountains. It is certainly true that the world's mountainous regions are generally much less **populated** than the lowlands. These regions are difficult to get to, and it's hard work walking uphill and downhill all the time! Nevertheless, some of our early human **ancestors** settled in the mountains. Perhaps they followed rivers upstream and uphill, so that they always had a constant supply of water. Later, people found that **settlements** built on high ground were easier to protect. Mountain settlers could see others coming and take action if they wanted to keep them away.

High up in the Andes Mountains, this Aymara woman rows her reed boat on Lake Titicaca. The shores of the lake were once part of the Inca Empire.

Ancient Andean cultures

People first settled in the Andes Mountains of South America many thousands of years ago. Their ancestors had traveled to North America from Asia and moved south. By about 5000 B.C.E. people were keeping some of the mountain animals that they had previously hunted, such as alpacas and llamas. They kept herds of animals near their settlements, which meant there was always a supply of milk and meat, as well as skins for clothing. Some people then began farming, growing corn and potatoes. By about 1000 B.C.E there was widespread settlement in the Andes.

Around Lake Titicaca

Lake Titicaca lies at a height of 12,500 feet (3,811 meters) above **sea level** in the Andes on the border between Peru and Bolivia. It is one of the highest lakes in the world. Its shores and islands are home to the Aymara people, who traditionally live by farming and fishing in the lake from boats made of reeds. The Aymara have lived here for many centuries, and some manage to carry on their traditional way of life today.

The Incas

The greatest of the ancient **Andean** cultures was the Inca **civilization.** They founded a capital at Cuzco around 1100 C.E. and developed from a small tribe into an organized people under one ruler. The Inca began to conquer neighboring lands until they ruled over a population of millions. Mountain **peaks** were sacred to the Incas, and they sometimes made human sacrifices in the high Andes.

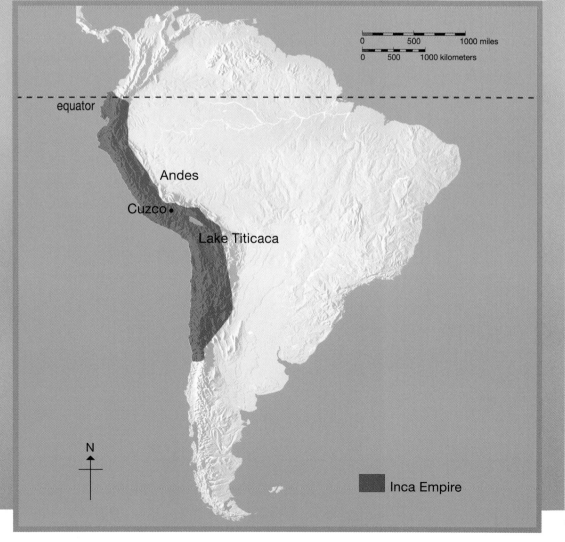

Mountain farmers

Farming in the mountains is hard work. The biggest problem is finding flat land for growing crops and grazing animals. The Incas (see page 19) overcame this problem by turning the slopes of the Andes into **terraces** of flat fields for farming. To do this they had to carry soil up from the **valleys** below. They laid the soil flat and built walls to protect their fields and stop them from slipping down the mountain slopes.

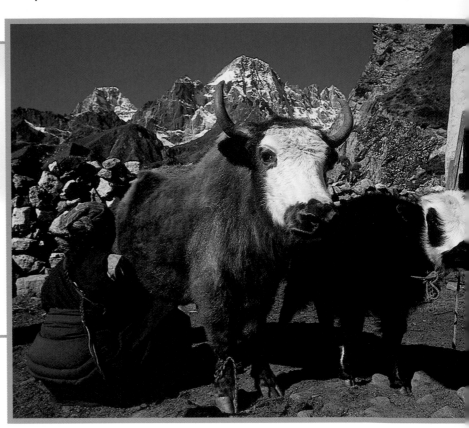

In the high Himalayas of Nepal, Sherpa villagers and farmers find yaks useful not only for their milk, which can be turned into butter, but also for their meat.

In the Himalayas

The mountain-dwelling Sherpa people of Nepal are used to life in the high Himalayas. Some of their villages are more than 11,500 feet (3,500 meters) above **sea level,** and they have summer **settlements** even higher up, where they live when the weather is warmer. The Sherpas raise yaks, and their farming villages are surrounded by terraced fields of barley, buckwheat, potatoes, and radishes. During the 1900s, many Sherpas used their knowledge of the Himalayan **peaks** to become mountaineering guides. In 1953 a Sherpa, Tenzing Norgay, was one of the first two men to climb to the top of Everest, the world's highest mountain.

Up and down the mountain

In the alpine regions of Switzerland, Austria, and other European countries, mountain farmers live by the seasons. In summer, when the grass is fresh and green, dairy farmers **graze** their cattle on the high **alpine meadows** above the farming villages. In the fall, before the first snows cover the meadows, the farmers bring their animals back down the mountain. The cattle spend winter inside sheds on the farm to protect them from the cold. The growth of **tourism** in the region means that this alpine farming is slowly dying out.

Rice terraces

The Ifugao people of northern Luzon, the largest island in the Philippines, are rice growers. They are famous for their terraced fields, surrounded by high stone walls, which cling to the slopes of their mountainous region. Some of the walls were built long ago by their **ancestors,** who learned how to bring water to the terraces through a clever system of pipes. They live in small villages of five to ten houses scattered among the fields.

Sun and snow

Weather changes are usually greater in the mountains than at lower levels. In many mountainous regions it is hot and sunny in the summer, but very cold in winter. This has a big effect on **tourism.** In summer, many people like to take their vacations in mountain towns and villages, where they can walk or hike and enjoy the beautiful scenery. In winter the hotels, guesthouses, and apartments in the same towns will be full of people who enjoy skiing and other winter sports. Many mountain resorts have **adapted** very successfully to this seasonal approach.

KITZBÜHEL SKI AREA

The town of Kitzbühel has a permanent population of just 8,200 people. Above the town there are 102 miles (164 kilometers) of ski runs, served by 59 ski lifts. On the map the black ski runs are difficult, the red are medium, and the blue runs are supposed to be easy—if you're a good skier!

A changing mountain town

The town of Kitzbühel, in the Austrian Alps, was founded in the 1100s. It once belonged to Bavarian dukes and bishops, who built a church there in 1373. In the 1500s nearby silver and copper mines made the townspeople wealthy. The last mine closed in 1770. The town probably changed little between then and the middle of the 1900s when Kitzbühel became famous as a growing ski resort. Today it is one of the most popular resorts, and many of the old buildings have been converted into hotels. Every year the town stages the Hahnenkamm downhill race, which is one of the most famous ski races in the world.

Mile High City

Because it stands at 5,300 feet (1,609 meters) above **sea level**, Denver, the capital of Colorado, is known as the "Mile High City." It was founded in the **foothills** of the Rocky Mountains during the **gold rush** of 1859, when people went there in search of gold and a fortune. Few **prospectors** made much money, but gold and silver were found in the mountains. Business grew and a railroad reached the town in 1870. Cattle and sheep **ranchers** settled beside the town, which by 1900 had more than 100,000 citizens. Since then, Denver has grown dramatically. Tourists come to visit the Rocky Mountain National Park with its lakes, fishing streams, and trails. Nearby ski resorts, such as Vail and Aspen, made the city even more popular. In 1995 Denver International Airport opened, helping business and tourism. The city now has a **population** of about half a million people.

The city of Denver is just southeast of Rocky Mountain National Park. It is less than 95 miles (150 km) away from the highest peak in the Rockies, Mount Elbert (14,400 ft/4,399 m).

Changing Mountains

Some of the world's most valuable resources come from mountains. For this reason, many mountain regions have become centers of **industry.**

Using fast-flowing rivers

The fast-flowing rivers of mountainous regions are useful for producing electricity. In the Snowy Mountains in southeast Australia, **dams** have been built on rivers so that water can be stored in **reservoirs.** Some of the water then flows down specially built tunnels and pipes. The water falls fast for hundreds of feet, driving **generators** to make electricity for Canberra, Australia's capital city. This industry changes the **landscape.** When dams are built, they flood **valleys,** destroying plants and other wildlife.

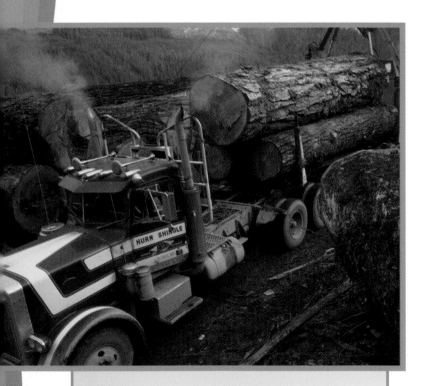

▲ The roots of trees help to hold soil in place, protecting it from the effects of weather. So when trees are cut down, there is a much greater rate of soil **erosion.**

Logging

Logging is the most important industry in many mountain areas. Thick forests of fir and other trees on the slopes of the Cascade **Range,** in the Pacific Northwest of the United States, are used to supply the timber industry. The mountain forests of the southeast Asian islands of Borneo and Sumatra are also being cut down for timber. This has threatened many rare mountain animals of the forests with losing their homes and perhaps even dying out.

Mining the mountains

Metals and minerals are common in mountain areas. There are huge mines in many of the world's major mountain ranges. The world's largest copper **strip mine** is in Chuquicamata, Chile (shown below). This mining town is on a **plateau** nearly 9,800 feet (3,000 meters) up in the Andes Mountains. Farther north in the Andes, there are many tin mines in Bolivia, where the mountains are also important for mining lead, silver, and zinc. These mines create huge holes in the ground. They bring wealth to a region, but they also have an big effect on the landscape. It is not always possible to fill in the mines when they are no longer useful.

Another change caused by logging, and all forms of industry, is road building. Workers need roads to take equipment up the mountain and bring down what they extract. Building roads means that more trees are cut down, other plants are destroyed, and soil is worn away. In many cases this leaves the slopes beside the roads bare and can lead to **landslides** and floods.

Cable cars and lifts

Skiing and other winter sports change mountain regions. One of the most obvious changes is the sight of cable cars and different forms of lifts, which take skiers and snowboarders up the mountains. In Kitzbühel (see page 22), for example, there are five cable cars. In 2002 the Winter Olympics were held on the mountain slopes near Salt Lake City, Utah, where many new runs and tracks were built for various winter sports.

Skiers enjoy the Snowy Mountains of northeast Victoria, Australia. These are the highest mountains in the Australian Alps.

Climbing and hiking

Mountaineering and rock climbing are popular sports. People enjoy the challenge of getting to the top of a mountain, often by the most difficult route. Today there are many adventure trips taken to remote mountain areas, such as the Andes and the Himalayas. Many people enjoy spending leisure time and vacations in the mountains, simply walking or hiking. All these activities have a big impact on mountains, as huts and even hotels are built for these adventurous mountaineers. Most do their best to leave the mountains as they found them, but changes to the natural environment are bound to occur.

Overusing the mountains

If too many people visit a mountain region, they can cause much damage. They might damage plants, and too many trampling feet can leave soil bare. The bare soil is then easily washed away by heavy rain. Skiing can have a similar effect, and skiing "off-piste" (that is, away from recognized, marked runs) can even disturb the snow and cause dangerous **avalanches.** Some other problems caused by tourists can be easily avoided. People should never leave litter, and they should be very careful with matches and campfires to make sure that they do not start forest fires.

Looking to the future

We all want to enjoy the mountains, but if we change them too much, there will be little left to enjoy. The governments of many countries tackle this problem by setting aside nature reserves and national parks, allowing local wildlife to thrive. These measures help mountain regions to go on developing and changing slowly and naturally. The forces of our planet ensure that, thousands of years from now, the world's mountains will look very different from the way they look today.

These rescue workers are searching for survivors after an avalanche at Galtür, in the Austrian Alps.

Mountain Facts and Figures

The world's longest mountain ranges

range	continent	length in miles	length in km
Andes	South America	4,474	7,200
Rockies	North America	2,983	4,800
Himalayas	Asia	2,361	3,800
Great Dividing Range	Australia	2,237	3,600
Transantarctic Mountains	Antarctica	2,175	3,500
Brazilian Coastal Range	South America	1,864	3,000
Sumatra-Java Range	Asia	1,802	2,900
Aleutian Range	North America	1,616	2,600
Tien Shan	Asia	1,367	2,200
New Guinea Range	Asia	1,243	2,000

The world's highest mountains (all in the Himalayas, Asia)

mountain	height in ft/m
Everest	29,078 / 8,863
K2	28,248 / 8,610
Kangchenjunga	28,208 / 8,598
Lhotse	27,923 / 8,511
Makalu	27,824 / 8,481
Dhaulagiri	26,795 / 8,167
Manaslu	26,758 / 8,156
Cho Oyu	26,748 / 8,153
Nanga Parbat	26,653 / 8,124
Annapurna	26,545 / 8,091

Highest mountains in each continent

mountain	continent	range	height in ft/m
Everest	Asia	Himalayas	29,078 / 8,863
Aconcagua	South America	Andes	22,835 / 6,960
McKinley (Denali)	North America	Alaska Range	20,321 / 6,194
Kilimanjaro	Africa	—	19,340 / 5,895
Elbrus	Europe	Caucasus	18,510 / 5,642
Vinson	Antarctica	Ellsworth	16863 / 5,140
Mount Kosciuszko	Australia	Great Dividing Range	7,310 / 2,228

La Paz, the capital of Bolivia, was built on the site of an ancient Inca village. It is in the Andes Mountains, and at 11,917 feet (3,632 meters), is the world's highest capital.

Worst avalanches of the 20th century

location	year	estimated deaths
Alps, Italy	1916	10,000
Huaraz, Peru	1941	5,000
Huascaran, Peru	1962	3,500
Chungar, Peru	1971	600
Blons, Austria	1954	411

Worst volcanic eruptions

location	year	estimated deaths
Tambora, Indonesia	1815	92,000
Miyi-Yama, Indonesia	1793	53,000
Mont Pelée, Martinique	1902	38,000
Krakatoa, Indonesia	1883	36,000
Nevado del Ruiz, Colombia	1985	23,000
Etna, Italy	1669	20,000
Vesuvius, Italy	79	20,000
Kelud, Indonesia	1586	10,000
Lamington, Papua New Guinea	1951	5,000

Glossary

adapt change to suit certain conditions

alpine meadow grassland on a high mountain, such as in the Alps of Europe

altitude height of a mountain (measured above sea level)

ancestor person who lived long ago, from whom someone is descended

Andean relating to the region of the Andes, a mountain range in South America

avalanche large fall of snow or rocks down a mountainside

boulder large stone that has been worn smooth

broad-leaved tree tree with wide, flat leaves instead of needles

chain group of mountain ranges

civilization advanced culture, or a people with an advanced culture

conifer tree with needlelike leaves that bears its seeds in cones

continent one of the world's seven huge land masses

crag steep, rugged rock

crust hard, outer layer of the earth

dam large barrier across a river that holds back water

erode slowly wear away. Soil and rocks are eroded by the effects of the weather.

fault crack in the earth's crust

foothills lower hills around the edge of a mountain range

generator machine that turns one form of energy, such as the power of water, into electricity

glacier slowly moving mass of ice

gold rush large numbers of people moving to a region where gold has been found

graze to eat growing grass, or to feed animals on grass

industry business, often factories that make things

landscape natural scenery

landslide large fall of soil or rocks down a mountainside

logging cutting down trees for timber

molten melted (turned into liquid by heat)

peak pointed top of a mountain

plateau flat area of high land

population total number of people who live in a particular place

predator animal that hunts and kills other animals for food

prospector person who explores a region for gold or other precious metal

rancher person who farms a cattle ranch

range series of mountains that form a group

reservoir human-made lake where water is collected and stored

Ring of Fire zone around the Pacific Ocean where there are many active volcanoes at the edge of plates

sea level level of the sea's surface, which is used as zero in calculating the height of a mountain

settlement place where people live permanently

snow line height on a mountain above which there is always snow

strata layers of rock

strip mine mine that is worked on, or just below, the surface rather than deep underground

tectonic plate huge piece of the earth's crust

terrace flat area of land cut into a slope to be used for growing things

tourism business of organizing holidays and visits to places of interest

tree line height on a mountain above which no tress grow

valley low area between mountains

volcano opening where molten rock and gas come from deep inside the earth, often forming a mountain

weathering wearing away of rocks by wind, rain, and ice

Further Reading

Chambers, Catherine. *Mapping Earthforms: Mountains*. Chicago: Heinemann Library, 2000.

Harris, Tim. *Biomes Atlases: Mountains*. Chicago: Raintree, 2003.

Oxlade, Chris. *Earth Files: Mountains*. Chicago: Heinemann Library, 2002.

Sauvain, Philip. *Geography Detective: Mountains*. London: Zoe Books, 1996.

Index

Franklin Pierce College Library

00147121

DATE DUE

APR 1 7 2008

GAYLORD

PRINTED IN U.S.A.